Daddy Doctor-Friends: Plus-Size Reverse Harem

Dolliana Jeffries

Published by Dolliana Jeffries, 2024.

Table of Contents

Daddy Biker-Friends: Plus-Size MMMF Why Choose Adults Short Story

Taboo MFMM Foursome Menage Age-Gap, MC OTT, Smutty RH Quick Read

DOLLIANA JEFFRIES[1]

1. https://www.amazon.com/s?k=dolliana+jeffries

Chapter 1

My dad's strict schedule always left me lonely and needing company. His being a single dad and me being an only child always made me resort to my wild imagination. At an early age, I'd imagined myself as a fairy and had always worked up stories in my head about my explorations.

As soon as I got older, those weren't the fantasies that plagued my mind. The ones that took residence became more intriguing and had taken effect as soon as I started reading steamy romance novels. That opened a whole new world for me and ever since, I'd been stuck, wishing I had the opportunity to be as adventurous.

My fantasies became even worse when my dad had long shifts at the hospital, and I had no choice but to go next door to the neighbor's house. Sylvia was a pretty, fun woman who always did her best to make sure I was comfortable, though the only company she provided was her own and her splurge of ongoing boyfriends. My father didn't know that part, as he was so busy, but I bet if he knew what I was exposed to at Sylvia's, my first day would have been my last.

I'd kept the secret to myself because somehow I was intrigued by the men who crooned after her now. I could see how full of life she was when each one came around, and I admired that. A few years ago, after her divorce, she was left an unfortunate and frustrated woman who was compensated by the large settlement her lawyer was able to squeeze from her ex-husband.

After, it was like something clicked in her, and she started to live her best life. I remember one of those nights when her new boy toy came over. He was younger than her, but despite her being thirty-four, he couldn't seem to keep his hands off her – sometimes, his hands would trail down her cleavage, and she would glance at me, swat at his hand and giggle. She always seemed keen on protecting my 'innocence,' even though I was nineteen years old at the time.

I could recall clearly one night when Conrad had come over – I stayed in the guestroom right next to theirs and could hear her jubilant giggles through the paper-thin walls. My eyes were wide open, staring at the ceiling fan that spun ever so slowly, adding to the agony I already felt.

I lay in bed with my ears peeled, hearing the giggles and the soft bumps of furniture until it all but stopped. For a second, I'd wondered if they'd left the room, but then I heard soft moans that got louder with each passing second. My heart lurched in my chest as soon as I figured out what it was, and my body was engulfed with heat.

Somehow, regardless of being in the other room, it felt like I was right there watching them. My stinging cheeks gave testament to that, and for a second, I imagined what it would be like to watch them. As the moans got louder and Conrad's name became a constant on Sylvia's lips, I could feel my body flooding with heat that settled right between my legs. There was a persistent need to touch myself, but it almost felt dirty to be doing so in someone's house.

I could feel the sin in my groin and a constant yearning that left me more desperate. I got up from the bed and silently walked out of the bedroom. I didn't even know what I expected to find or do from my stroll, but when I saw Sylvia's bedroom door slightly cracked open, my heart hammered in my chest as a thought came to me.

As I peeped through the crack, I could see a clear view of the bed and them on it. It felt like I was about to faint with the pleasure rushing through me – seeing the way Sylvia had her legs wide open while Conrad thrust in and out of her. With each thrust of his hips, she moaned, her hands reaching out to grab him and anchor him in place.

I used my index finger to push the door open a tad wider, knowing that if either one of them turned their heads, they'd maybe see me. But they were lost in each other, and the last thing they had their minds on was an open door. I was burning up, my lungs almost left dry as I listened to Sylvia's cries of pleasure. The more she cried, the faster Conrad went until he grunted and pulled out of her. I swallowed hard, biting down on my gasp when his thick cock slid from her. The dim lighting in the room robbed me of the details, but I could clearly see that he was huge and thick, and somehow, that realization made me even hotter.

He slapped himself on Sylvia as her chest rose and fell rapidly in her chest. I thought he was going to finish off, but then Sylvia switched positions, going on her knees with her back arched in front of him. Conrad massaged her ass cheeks, spreading them apart and muttering something indecipherable before he plunged into her from behind. Sylvia's scream pierced the room, and I knew that by now, she had completely forgotten that she had a guest in the house. Not that I minded – I didn't want them to spare me. I enjoyed every bit of it.

My arousal became almost crippling, and I couldn't help myself. I pressed my back against their bedroom wall and slid down to a squatting position. I fumbled as I slipped my fingers under my nightgown and then beneath my panties. As soon as my middle finger touched my clit, I closed my eyes as the bolt of pleasure rushed through me. I was soaking wet, and I found myself flicking my hands over and over the little wet knob, which was well hidden by my pussy's thick hooded lips.

But that couldn't quell the burning desire that pumped hotly through my veins. I needed to feel a greater sense of satisfaction, and so I dipped my fingers inside my pussy, felt myself cream against my fingers and began to fill myself while listening to Sylvia and Conrad's moans and grunts.

I was lost in the pleasure – my ass now crushed against the floor while I pumped my fingers in and out of my quim. I squeezed my eyes shut, feeling the pleasure that settled in my gut. Over time, the sounds of Sylvia and Conrad faded in the background, and all I could focus on was my own pleasure.

It felt like my heart was going to burst out of my chest, and I couldn't do anything to stop it. I clenched my teeth together, biting down harshly on my lips as the feeling intensified.

"Celine." It took me a second to realize it was my name being called.

I stiffened as my eyes popped open, and I focused my gaze on Sylvia and Conrad standing right in front of me. A chill ran down my spine that dampened the heat that engulfed my body.

I adjusted myself in such a way that my nightdress would obscure my cunt from their gaze with my fingers still pasted to my flesh. I sat frozen as I stared up at the intrigued looks on their flushed faces. I burned red.

"I-" I sought words to say, but there was nothing I could say to make this less embarrassing. Still, regardless of being caught, I couldn't seem to tear my gaze away from Conrad's long cock that dangled in front of me – still drenched with Sylvia's juices.

I swallowed hard. "I'm sorry..." I said, my voice barely above a whisper.

I'd expected outrage, but up until now, nothing in their demeanors resembled anything of the sort.

"So you like to listen, huh?" Sylvia began. "What do you think about watching?" she asked, and my pulse quickened.

Never in my wildest imaginations did I imagine this taking such a turn. Yet I couldn't help myself, the request filled me with so much desire that all I could do in that moment was nod yes.

"Yes, please..."

Conrad reached for my hand and pulled me up. My knees buckled as I stood and followed behind him, his taut buttocks a sight as we moved inside. My heart was still hammering, and for a second, I thought this was all a dream, but as soon as my ass hit the cool sofa at the side of the room, I knew it was real.

Sylvia smiled at me and resumed her position on the bed. Conrad climbed after her, his eyes never leaving her naked back. They both glanced at me before Conrad raised Sylvia's legs, pressing them to her chest and granting me a view of her wet, plump pussy.

Conrad's Adam's apple bobbed as he got himself comfortable, his length pointing right at her passage. He lowered himself, and I watched with bated breath as he pierced her with his firmness. I swallowed hard, getting even more aroused by

Sylvia's soulful moans. I licked my lips as my fingers inched closer to my open legs.

My cheeks still stung with heat, but I could throw my pride through the window if it meant getting to experience something as sweet as this. They invited me in – that alone should tell me that they were fine with everything, and I shouldn't be feeling so tense.

I glued my eyes to the sight of their bodies joining, Conrad's length more flushed with Sylvia's juices each time he went inside her. Quickly, his pace increased, and I held my breath as the sounds of their pleasure thrummed against my eardrums. I couldn't get enough – for a moment, I wished that it was me in their position, but at the same time, I also loved watching. There was just something very arousing about watching someone having sex in real life that I couldn't quite explain.

He drilled her hard and deep, taking his time to make sure she felt everything he had to offer. My fingers found my crotch again, and I almost shuddered as soon as I touched my sensitive flesh. My digits slipped further down and found my slobbering passage again. I gasped as I sunk them in and realized they'd heard because Conrad glanced at me and smiled while he continued to fuck Sylvia hard.

I began to thrash my pussy harder and faster, feeling the pleasure build in my loins. I was so close, and I didn't want to stop. Sylvia and Conrad seemed to be nearing an end, too, and I kept up the same pace as they did, wishing it was a real cock filling me but still loving the feel of my own fingers.

With a grunt, Conrad stiffened, and Sylvia cried out. I watched as my fingers moved at the speed of light. His cock swelled halfway inside her, and with a sigh, he came, filling her up to the point where his cum spilled from her pussy.

I sucked in a breath and clamped my eyes tightly shut, trying to make sense of all the pleasure I was experiencing. It grew tenfold, and with a small cry, I came, my pussy convulsing around my fingers. All I felt was the feeling of being on cloud nine, accompanied by warm wetness that soaked both my dress and the sofas.

It was too much.

I blacked out.

Chapter 2

IT HAD BEEN A YEAR since that night at Sylvia's, and I couldn't seem to get it out of my mind even now. That was the closest I ever went to having my fantasies fulfilled, and I couldn't believe that it was now a year later and even more unbelievable, I was still a virgin.

It wasn't because I didn't have men wanting to do the deed with me, but what I wanted required three specific men, and I was hellbent on having nothing at all if I couldn't have them. A year ago, I'd thought that the man to take my virginity would be Conrad since he was so skilled and open-minded, but shortly after that steamy encounter that night, he and Sylvia ended things, and he moved to a new state. I never saw him after that, but it was like the stars were aligning for me because I had my sights set on three other men who I believed would give me the best time ever if the opportunity ever arose.

Just thinking about them made me hot and ready to be pounded into next year.

"Hey, Celine, ready to go?" Sylvia asked as she grabbed her keys from the table and walked past me to the front door.

"Yeah, I can't wait to see it actually."

Her bright-red lips stretched into a smile. "You should have seen it sooner, but I know how your dad is."

I resisted the urge to roll my eyes as we moved to the car. "Yeah, my dad has me on a tight leash these days, but he's just overprotective."

"Yeah, being the overprotective parent never works. My parents were like that, and yet I had boyfriends sneaking in every week," she winked as she started the engine of the car.

I was smiling hard. "Boyfriends, huh?"

She smiled. "Men have always been my weakness, sweetheart."

I giggled. "Knowing what I know about you now, I'm surprised you were even married."

She grinned. "I don't know what got into me. I guess I thought I was in love. I was young and foolish."

I relaxed in my seat. "I want to be married someday."

She scoffed. "Says the little minx who wants three men fucking her guts out."

My mouth fell open. It was no surprise to have Sylvia talk to me this way, but most times, her words still somehow managed to shock me. After that night, we had grown more comfortable with each other, and Sylvia had taught me about things no book had ever come close to. She was like my best friend, even though she was fifteen years older than me.

"It's modern times; I'm sure relationships like that aren't weird now."

"Yeah, definitely. And who knows, love, the strip club will have an after-dark session. Maybe your fantasies aren't so far off," she winked.

My brows furrowed. "After dark? You never mentioned this."

"Yeah, well, I was waiting for us to arrive at the club first, but since we're on the topic," she shrugged, glancing at me to see my expression.

My mouth was hung open. "That sounds exciting. So what? People get to have sex with who they want?"

"Yeah, stuff like that. People will be there watching – it's a whole thing."

My cheeks burned hot. "You know I'll never be brave enough for things like that," I mumbled.

She scoffed. "You have too many wild fantasies to still be a shy girl, Celine."

I knew that was true.

"But I don't want to have sex with just strangers. I want it to be with people I know," I explained. "People I actually like."

"Like who? Your dad's friends?"

My entire body became heated. There was not a single thing about me that Sylvia didn't know. I felt comfortable talking to her and only her. While I was considered a mostly shy girl, Sylvia knew exactly what this shy girl wanted.

I shrugged. "I suppose that was a stretch, wasn't it?"

"Of course not. It isn't a hard thing to seduce men, Celine, you know that. Plus, you're a beautiful girl with curves to kill – what man wouldn't want you?" she said as she quickly gave me a once-over.

"My dad's friends," I emphasized with the raise of a brow.

Sylvia rolled her eyes. "All you need is the right moment; I can tell you that much."

I sighed lightly, relaxing in the seat and pondering on her words. As much as I would have liked to believe her, I just knew that my fantasies were too wild to become reality.

WHEN WE ARRIVED AT the new strip club Sylvia had opened up, she was beaming with pride, looking between me and the shop as she gauged my expression. I smiled hard, looking at the black-painted brick walls and the huge red sign that spelled 'Club Enigma' above the entrance.

"I can't believe I'm actually seeing it in person," I said, glancing at Sylvia. "It's just like you envisioned it in your mind, isn't it?"

She nodded.

"It's beautiful," I said truthfully.

"Well, your approval is all that matters anyway," she said so casually without even knowing how much that meant to me.

"You mean that?" I couldn't help but ask.

"Of course I do. I mean, the age gap is huge, but I consider you one of my closest friends, so you mean a lot to me."

My cheeks became heated. "You honestly mean a lot to me, too."

She winked. "I'm glad the day your dad asked me to keep an eye out for you. To be honest, at first, I wasn't even too enthusiastic about it, but as we spent more time together, I was happy he did."

I grinned. "Me too."

We moved inside the club. "Now, if your dad knew what's been happening, that would be the end of it. As a matter of fact, I have no idea how he'll take the news of me opening a strip club, of all things."

I giggled, though I knew the situation was more serious than I let on. I didn't want my dad to know about this because I knew, despite our friendship with Sylvia, he would see her in a new light. For as long as I could, I'd kept Sylvia's promiscuity on the downlow, but that was behind closed doors. As the owner of a strip club, she would be right there for John Public to see, and it would only be a matter of time before he knew.

Even the thought of it sent a feeling of dread rushing down my spine. I was an adult, but whatever my dad says always goes. It had been like that for the longest while, and I really didn't have a problem with it. Now, things were changing.

My thoughts came to a halt as soon as I stepped inside the air-conditioned club and saw the glistening floors, the dark walls and the bar stacked with liquor. The space was huge, and poles were lined throughout on small pedestal-like structures.

Seeing it for the first time caused my heart to swell in my chest, as this was something Sylvia and I had been talking about for a few months now. We'd looked at the plan together and sometimes, I'd even help her choose a few things. However, she'd always kept the location from me until now, and it did not disappoint. It felt like my very own achievement.

I moved towards her and hugged her tight. "I swear it's perfect; I'm so proud of you."

She rubbed my back before she pulled back and smiled, her eyes glistening. "Thanks, sweetheart."

I watched as she strutted towards the bar with her creamy long legs that she always joked would reach the sky. She was such a delicate woman – and a feminine one at that, too. Sylvia looked like the type to be on the front page of a magazine with her beauty and slenderness. For a long time, I'd wished that was me, but she had always reassured me that I was perfect the way I was – with all my curves that she sometimes joked about being envious of.

Of course, I knew it was a joke, but I'd finally grown to accept that Sylvia and I had two different body types, and I loved mine as much as she loved hers.

"So I have a bartender that's coming in a few – she should be here soon. If you'd like to know anything, you can ask her since I won't be here most of the time."

I was about to ask why when I remembered Sylvia would be gone in a few days to do business.

"Yeah, I think I'll be here most nights when my dad has late shifts too."

Sylvia smiled. "I hope so."

Skye came, and we chatted for a while. She was a friendly girl who was on the slender side and always kept complimenting me about how sexy my curves were – even that I could work there as a stripper – which served as a huge joke for Sylvia and I, who laughed about it for about a minute. Sylvia also gave us some tips on business, and I remembered she said something that stuck. She'd told me that the trick of the trade wasn't bringing in the customers; it was in keeping them and making them spend money. The longer the clients stayed, the more money she made. I couldn't wait to see how true that was.

Chapter 3

I LEFT THE CLUB LATER that evening and headed straight home. I was shocked to find my dad there. I'd expected him a bit later, but here he was, cooking up something in the kitchen.

I smiled, trying to seem as casual as ever as I approached him. "Hey, Dad," I announced from behind.

Without looking, he answered. "Hey, sweetheart. Where have you been?" he asked.

I cleared my throat, leaning against the counter. "Sylvia and I made a quick run into town."

With that, he paused the stir-fry he was making, placed the fork on the counter and wiped his hand into a towel. His piercing blue eyes were always intimidating, but I'd grown used to them over time. Still, my heart raced a little – this wasn't usually his response to me hanging out with Sylvia.

"I heard she opened up a strip club in town..." he said. My pulse quickened. So much for holding off on the info for as long as I could.

I cleared my throat and reached into the refrigerator to get some water. "Yeah, she did actually."

His thick brows rose slightly. "I was surprised when I heard. She never struck me as the type."

"The type to do what?" I asked.

"Open up a business like that. As a matter of fact, I had no idea she was business-minded."

"Yeah."

He stared at me for a couple of seconds. "I don't want you hanging around there, though," he said before turning to continue with his cooking.

I was taken aback, though I knew it was something to be expected. "Dad, I'm an adult now, you know," I pointed out.

"Trust me, I know, but still, those aren't places you want to spend your time."

My lips parted to contest that, but instead, I settled on a simple, "Okay."

"Could you set the table for me, please? The guys are coming over."

My brows perked up, and my heart lurched in my chest. "Really?"

He chuckled. "Yes, really. It's been a while since we sat here and chatted, hasn't it?"

I nodded as I moved towards the cabinets. "It has."

"With me being director of the hospital, I hardly get the time, so I'm making the best of it since Jensen and the others are also off this evening."

I smiled. "Most times, they're off, though."

"Yeah, they get to go home at night – that isn't always the case for me as you know."

I nodded. "I know."

He glanced at me, his expression softening. "You're okay with my new role, right? I mean, it has been over a year now, but sometimes I have to ask since it's always been just me and you from the beginning of time."

"Dad, I'm fine. You've always wanted this, and you know I'm proud of you."

He pulled in a breath. "Yeah, but we hardly get to talk like old times. Sometimes, it feels like I'm missing out, y'know?"

I shook my head. "Trust me, I'm fine. I miss you sometimes, of course, but I'm a big girl now, and I know what this is all about."

"You're heading off to college next year, too. We'll hardly get to see each other then, too."

I scratched my neck. "Yeah, off to another state. I don't think I'm ready," she chuckled.

He grinned. "I don't think I am either. Do you regret taking the year off?"

"Definitely not."

We both laughed. Once I was done setting the table, it dawned on me that my father's friends would be here soon, and I was a mess.

I cleared my throat and turned to my dad. "I'm gonna go and freshen up. I'll be back."

"Okay, sweetheart."

I quickly ran upstairs and headed for the bathroom. I took a quick shower while thinking about how the entire dinner would go. I'd known them for almost a year now, and though I didn't see them as often as I'd hoped, we still had a fairly good relationship. All of them were cool people – definitely cooler than my dad, who was stricter than all of them together.

Once I finished taking a shower, I began to mull over what I would wear. Something out of the ordinary would definitely have my dad lifting a brow, so I opted for what I usually wore, which was leggings and a t-shirt. I was getting dressed when I heard their cars pulling up outside. Soon after, the doorbell rang, and my heart began to plunder in my chest, my palms gone sweaty as a wave of nerves passed through my body.

I pulled in a breath and stared at myself in the mirror. I used my hands to sweep my loose hair back and reached for my lip gloss as soon as I saw how dry my lips were.

I rubbed my hands along my thighs before I left the room, feeling more anxious the further I walked and started to hear their voices. Hector's deep, bass voice was the first thing I heard as soon as I reached the stairs. Then, it was Milano's soft chuckle. I couldn't help the flutter in my stomach – the warmth that sizzled through my veins.

They were all gathered in the dining room, not far from the table which I'd set. Dad was serving them scotch. Seeing them triggered something in me which was more than just sexual. They were all so huge and tall – more like lumberjacks instead of doctors – all with beards.

"Hey, guys," I announced as I entered the room, a huge smile on my face.

All their gazes shifted in my direction, smiles splitting their faces as soon as I saw them.

"Celine – it's been ages," Milano said.

I smiled. "You're telling me. You guys are the ones who've been strangers," I teased.

Hector chuckled. "We'll take that. It's nice seeing you, though," he said.

I met his grey eyes and smiled at him. "Likewise."

"You look as beautiful as ever, Celine," Jensen chipped in, taking a sip of his scotch while he watched me from over the rim of his glass. His scorching gaze caused the flesh between my inner thighs to tingle and I cleared my throat, reminding myself that my dad was here.

A few minutes later, we were all seated at the table. Everyone helped themselves to the food, and I felt like a kid in a candy shop, surrounded by all these beautiful men – seated right between Jensen and Milano around the small circular table they all seemed to fill up with their domineering sizes.

I dug into my food, wanting something to distract me from them. "The food tastes amazing, Dad," I said, glancing at him. He smiled at that.

"Sure does. This could be like a second career, Peter," Milano joked.

Dad scoffed. "I already have my plate full at the hospital."

"Definitely. It's not easy being the medical director of the biggest hospital in New York," Jensen said as he picked up a forkful of food.

"Yeah, it's not easy being a doctor overall. I don't know how you guys do it," I said.

Hector smiled. "Sometimes, I wonder the same thing, but we all love what we do. That's the fun part."

The others nodded in agreement.

"How about you, Celine? Ever considered coming into the field?"

I scoffed. "Not for a minute. I can barely stand the sight of my own blood."

They laughed.

"So, what are you studying in college next year?"

"Business," I informed.

"I hope Sylvia wasn't the one who convinced you on that one," my dad said.

I shot him a deadpan look but knew he was joking. "Dad, you know I always wanted to own my own business someday."

"I know sweetheart."

"Who's Sylvia?" Hector asked.

"She lives across from here. You know, the lady Celine is always with most times," Milano offered.

"Hector's eyes widened. "Ohh, gotchya."

"I heard she opened up a strip club in town," Jensen said.

I raised a brow. "Wow, news flies fast."

"Yeah, well, when it's good news like that, it's bound to fly fast."

Milano laughed. "Good news, huh?"

"Sure is. The other club is like miles away."

"True," Milano agreed.

"I doubt you guys will even have the time to go," I said, wanting to see their reaction. "When you're done working, wouldn't you all be too tired?"

"Never tired enough to see some ass shaking," Milano grinned.

"Come on," my dad scolded, glancing from them to me.

Milano laughed. "Loosen up a bit, Pete, Celine is twenty years old. I'm sure she's familiar with the term."

I shook my head.

We continued to eat until Dad suggested we go to the living room to relax. He took a seat in his recliner, his feet up. Milano and Jensen sat beside me while Hector occupied another seat. I knew it was a bad idea from the very moment I sat and smelt their musky perfumes that invaded my senses right away. Plus, Milano and Jensen were huge and with me being plus-sized, seated in the middle, there was barely enough room. Their hands were touching mine, and for a second, I wondered if their sitting here was deliberate. Did they want to sit beside me? Did they want to touch me.

I wanted to believe that more than anything, but as I glanced at them, I realized they didn't seem to have the slightest bit of interest in me or what I was about. Their gazes were glued to the television, and for a second, that dampened my spirits but not my desire. With their bodies this close to mine, I couldn't concentrate on much – more so football that I didn't even like. All I could think about was the now and how hot I felt with my body brushing against theirs. My flesh pooled with heat, and there was this constant need to touch myself, but I knew I definitely couldn't do that now – as much as I wanted to.

Jensen shifted a little, and I bit down on my lips so as not to respond – moan even. I was drenched with heat and could feel my armpits and palms begin to get sweaty again.

Thinking I couldn't handle it for another second, I got up and excused myself from the room. I quickly headed to the powder room close to the stairs, sighing heavily as I closed the door. Without thinking twice, I shoved my leggings down to my knees and stuffed my hands down my panties. The warm wetness of my arousal welcomed me as soon as my fingers touched my flesh. I bit down on my lips in an attempt to hold back my moans and slid my finger over my sensitive, wet bud. My knees buckled as a wave of arousal swept across me. I closed my eyes to bask in the moment while I used my fingers to pleasure myself, wishing it was either one of the men in my living room.

My digits were soaked with my wetness, my mouth almost salivating as I stood there, pleasuring myself. The more I thought about Jensen, Milano and Hector, the more the pleasure became more intense. I slid my fingers into my hole, pushing it as far as it could go and enjoying the feel of my pussy clinging to every thrust.

A moan slipped out, and I quickly clamped my lips together, making sure to not get another one out. The pressure began to build in my loins, and I knew it wouldn't be long before I came. I could almost taste my orgasm as it rushed to the forefront, desperate to give me release.

The door was pulled open, and I gasped when I saw Milano standing there. His eyes widened, and his lips parted to speak, but he was obviously in shock as he stared at me, his eyes lowering to where I had my hand buried.

"Fuck, Celine, I'm sorry. I didn't know anyone was in here," he said, swallowing, his Adam's apple bobbing.

I was in shock, too – this was the last thing I expected to happen, and a crippling feeling of fear rushed through me. I didn't know what I expected Milano to do, but I'd expected him to shut the door by now or leave, but he didn't. He just stood there staring.

With my heart thrumming, I pulled my fingers from my crotch, not anticipating the small sigh that escaped my lips.

His green eyes darkened to slits. "Do you want help with that?"

In my dreams, this would happen, but not in reality. This must be a joke, but the seriousness on his face told me it wasn't.

I nodded timidly, taking a step back into the small bathroom. Without even looking back, Milano entered and quickly closed the door behind him. it felt like I would pass out from the adrenaline rushing through my veins. Part of me still couldn't accept this as the truth, but I knew I would surely take advantage of every second of this.

I had no idea what Milano would do, so when he kissed me hard and deep, I whimpered from the sheer joy and unexpectedness of the situation. I clung to him and kissed him back the best I knew how, though I could feel the experience on his lips as he molded his lips unto mine, pulled at my tongue and suckled on my plump lips as if he'd known it forever. I could feel myself flooding with even more heat as he kissed me – my pussy pulled with more heat and arousal for him, ready to be touched. The roughness of Milano's beard created a bit of contrast from his hot lips. The ruggedness left me even more heady and disoriented.

Milano pulled apart for a brief second to meet my gaze. "This is so wrong, Celine, but fuck if I could just turn a blind eye to all this." With that said, he kissed me yet again, causing my knees to buckle, but his strong arm quickly slipped around to the small of my back and held me in place.

I propped my leg up on the toilet, spreading myself for him, given the circumstances. His warm hand found my naked skin, and as soon as his fingers touched me, I whimpered. It felt like his fingertips were laced with fire that spread throughout my skin at the single touch. He trailed his large hand up and down my legs before he slipped it between my thighs. He was just inches away from touching me, and I crooned like a baby for his touch.

When his firm fingers finally found my aching flesh, I leaned into him, desperate for his kisses even more while he flicked my clit with his finger. His finger drove back and forth in my slit, and I couldn't help my small moans as I kissed him. I could hear the sounds of my wet flesh contesting with the sloppy sounds of our kisses and that made me even wetter. My mouth opened up when he slipped his finger in, and my flesh clenched around it, wrapping it tight as it breached my folds and entered my cavern. Milano groaned then, slipping his finger farther before he came to a halt.

With his single finger still lodged inside me, he broke the kiss and met my gaze. I knew what he discovered, and my pulse quickened, waiting for his response.

"You're a virgin." It was more a statement than anything else. I didn't know what to concentrate on, my response to him or the fact that in the midst of all of this, his finger was where it needed it to be.

"Please don't stop," I said in what sounded like a whisper.

Milano took a second before his finger started to slide back and forth inside me again. My mouth fell open, and I clung to him, staring into his deep grey eyes as he filled me with his strokes.

Gradually, his pace quickened, and I bit down on my lips, not knowing what to make of myself. I was burning up, and with every stroke, I tipped closer and closer to the edge.

Milano drove his finger a bit deeper, and I stiffened, biting painfully hard on my lips to the point where I tasted the metallic taste of blood in my mouth. I quivered, my walls clenched down on Milano's finger tightly, my juices drenching his digits. He held me at the nape of my neck, pried my neck backward, and kissed me hard. Another moan threatened to spill, but I held back before it left my lips.

I was still a mess even seconds later when my quivers lessened. The euphoric feeling that rushed through me was too intense to bear. It wasn't just an orgasm – but an orgasm I had with Milano – the first man to touch me so intimately.

I swallowed, and my throat seemed parched. As the haze cleared from my mind, it then occurred to me where I was, and my stomach filled with panic.

"Shit," I hissed.

He finally withdrew his fingers, and I blushed neon when I saw how drenched they were with my juices.

Milano only smiled. "Satisfied?"

I licked over my lips and tried my best to meet his gaze. "For now."

His eyes darkened once again. "Maybe we can pick up where we left off some time?"

I nodded, taking a step back to pull up my leggings. "Yeah."

His eyes did one last quick scan of me before he adjusted his button-down shirt and reached for the knob.

"I'll go first," he said before flashing me one last smile and leaving the room.

I sighed heavily once he was gone, still finding it hard to come to terms with what had happened. I couldn't believe it – more so the fact that it happened while my dad and the others were in the next room. My heart was beating so fast any other surprise would give me a heart attack. I carefully and slowly collected myself, reveling in the aftermath of my orgasm – still somehow able to feel the after-effects of Milano's fingers inside me.

I washed my face and sighed at how reddened and flushed my reflection was. I gave myself another minute before I left the room, hoping I didn't look as disoriented as I felt.

When I entered the living room again, Milano was the first person I saw, and I was shocked to find that he was laughing and chatting with the others like nothing had happened.

"Everything okay, Sweetheart?" my dad asked, and I almost jumped out of my skin. Fortunately, I didn't react.

I only smiled. "Yeah, everything's great."

I glanced at Milano, who flashed me a small smile and rubbed his beard. It all brought me back to what had happened moments ago, and I couldn't help my blush.

Chapter 4

I WAS STILL HUMMING with happiness even the next day –
my mind still stuck on what had happened at my house. Even if
having them all to myself seemed like a stretch, at least now I was
certain that Milano wanted me. If he was the only one I had, I'd
still be a happy girl.

After my dad left for work, I went to Sylvia's since it would be
the last day I saw her until she left. She was on her way out when
I arrived, so I hopped in her car and drove with her to the club.
I was beaming, almost bursting with excitement to tell her about
what had happened. But I didn't even have to tell her – as soon as
she took a good glance at me, she could tell there was something
I wanted to say.

"Well, spill it already," she laughed. "I already know there's
something you want to say."

I adjusted myself in the seat before I replied, telling her all
about what happened last night. Once I was done talking, my
face burned with heat, awaiting a response from Sylvia.

"Wow, girl, you're bolder than I thought." She had a pleased
smile on her face that triggered my own.

"I didn't even know I had it in me. It just kinda happened," I
admitted a bit shyly.

"See, I told you men can't resist you; you're a bombshell."

I grinned. "I don't even know what will happen next. Do you think Milano will want to do this again, even though he said so, or will he come to his senses and start to think logically?" I asked.

Sylvia glanced at me. "He'll want more, trust me."

"How do you know that?"

"Because all he did was finger you. I'm sure he's dying to have something else inside you."

My stomach fluttered. "Maybe. Shit, I can't believe all this is happening. What about the others, though? Do you think they'll come around?"

Sylvia shrugged. "I don't know, baby, but have some faith. You'll get what you want eventually."

I didn't know how true that was, and maybe Sylvia was right. Maybe I didn't have enough faith to envision my fantasies becoming reality with the others as well. But the bright side was, if Milano managed to surrender himself, then maybe it would be just as easy for the others to do the same.

When we arrived at the bar, Skye was there preparing for the night ahead. She smiled as soon as she saw me, and I smiled back, giving her a gentle wave as I approached.

"Hey, you're here earlier than I expected," Sylvia said rounding the counter to help out.

"Yeah, tonight's gonna be a busy night. I have to have everything ready."

Sylvia grinned. "That's the spirit, love. I'll call the others later today as well. We're gonna need all hands on deck."

I picked at my nails as I watched them. "I could help out too y'know," I suggested.

Skye glanced at Sylvia, who glanced at me. "Definitely not, this is your first night, and you're gonna enjoy yourself. Plus, if your dad happens to pop by, I don't want him to see you behind a counter serving drinks." She raised a brow at that.

I scoffed. "You're probably right, even though he'll be at work."

"Can't run any risks, honey. I'm surprised he didn't accost me about opening a strip club with you in my company."

I giggled. "He was surprisingly more chill about the situation than I expected."

Sylvia raised a brow. "Damn, well, maybe miracles do happen after all."

Skye giggled. "Your dad is that strict, huh?" she asked as she wiped a glass dry.

"More than you know," I said.

She nodded. "You're an adult, right?"

"Yeah, I'll be twenty-one in a few months."

"Damn, dads can be such pains in the ass sometimes."

I smiled despite myself. "He's always been like that. I guess I'm kinda used to it by now."

Skye offered a knowing look.

"I'll be around back in the office, guys if you need me," Sylvia said as she already started to leave. I nodded and watched as she left, contemplating whether or not I should follow her. Skye seemed cool, but I just didn't know if I was capable of holding down a convo all by myself without Sylvia in the room.

"You look tense, Celine," she said, looking at me from under her eyes.

I immediately shifted positions. "I'm fine."

"Want a drink?... On me."

I bit down on my lips and glanced in the direction Sylvia had walked. Of course, she wouldn't have a problem with me taking a drink, but I also wondered if it was the right thing to do.

"Sure," I smiled.

She reached beneath the counter and took up a glass and a mixer. She poured some liquor in and a type of puree before she mixed it all together and served it in a glass.

I smiled and said my thanks as she handed it to me, taking a sip.

My brows perked up as soon as it hit my tongue, and my gaze flashed to Skye. The taste was almost sweet and fruity but with the right kick of liquor that added the extra punch.

"Wow, this actually tastes good. What is it?"

She had a smug smile on her face. "I call it the wet pussy cocktail..." her gaze shifted to the drink in my hand. "See that pinkish color."

My gaze dropped to the glass as well, and I snorted out a laugh. "That's creative as hell, and it tastes damn good, too."

"Hence the name," she winked.

I was cheesing hard, even more so as I drank more of the drink. With just one, I'd already started to feel all giggly and knew that would be about it.

Skye and I chatted for a bit, and I realized many thanks were due to the cocktail she'd served. That had managed to loosen my tongue a bit and, according to Skye, made me less tense.

We chatted and laughed – both Skye and Sylvia teaching me the trick of the trade – before I finally decided to head home and take a nap before I got ready for later in the night.

BEING AT HOME ONLY emphasized how lonely I was. And no, it wasn't a case of missing my dad and wanting someone to watch movies with. I wanted someone who would be all over me twenty-four-seven, getting to know every inch of my body while I got to know them. I wanted the full experience of having a man, but I was still intent on my earlier decision of not being with anyone if it wasn't one or all three of my father's friends.

I was still dying to hear back from Milano – waiting for the moment for us to 'pick up where we left off', but I didn't want to go running after him seeking answers and asking about his next move. Sylvia had taught me a long time ago that if a man were serious enough, he'd do all the chasing. And right now, I could only wonder if that was the case with Milano.

With a sigh, I got up several hours later and headed for the shower. I got dressed in a leather skirt and a low-cut top that did much to amplify my generous cleavage. I let my hair out, pleased with my lustrous dark curls, and then I left for the club.

This was my first time being at any sort of club, and if this wasn't Sylvia's, I maybe would have spun the car around and headed back home. The line outside was never-ending – people eager to get inside, some jamming to the echoing music playing inside while they patiently waited. I stepped out of the car and immediately texted Sylvia that I was outside. There was no way I could wait in such a long line when I was almost struggling to keep up in the four-inch heels I wore.

She texted about a minute later with instructions to go around the back, and as soon as I got there, a bouncer was there to let me in. I stepped inside the room, seeing the strippers who looked at me as if I were a complete stranger – which, in truth, I was. That didn't stop them from getting dressed – not at all fazed that I was there seeing their nakedness. But why would they be anyway when over a hundred people would be seeing them in close to nothing?

I managed a smile as I slowly made my way through, almost bumping into Sylvia, who had a huge smile on her face. I was grinning with her.

"You look so fucking good, Celine," she said, looking at me from head to toe with a look of awe on her face.

I beamed. "Thank you."

"Fuck, you should wear leather more often. Damn girl, those curves are sex-xy!"

I giggled over the blasting hip-hop music. "Thank you, thank you." I stepped into the main hall with Sylvia at my arm, and my mouth fell open. I glanced at Sylvia, who only beamed with pride, not at all surprised by my reaction.

"Damn, this place is packed!" I exclaimed.

"It's fucking crazy, right!" she squealed.

I crashed into her arms as I gave her a hug. "This is dope. I'm proud of you."

"Thanks, my sweet girl. Now, come on, go get yourself something to drink and enjoy yourself. You can go crash in VIP. I already reserved a spot for you."

"What? Special treatment."

"Only the best for the best."

"Okay, you'll be busy, so I guess I'll see you around," I giggled.

Sylvia patted me on the shoulder and ushered me into the sea of people who congregated inside. I pushed my way through, spilling a thousand *I'm sorry's* as I bored my way through. No one seemed interested in me or what I had to say, though. They were all so engrossed in the music and the strippers who were on the stage.

I climbed the small stairs to VIP, which, to my surprise, was almost as packed as general but definitely more spacious and organized. There, I could see a full view of what was happening below – the strippers who were surrounded by women and men alike, staring at them shamelessly with paper notes waving in their hands. The dancer was a young girl – definitely older than me but still young. She was slender and petite, dressed in clothes that only covered her crotch and her nipples. Her skin seemed glazed with something as it glistened under the spotlight right above her. She caressed the pole as if it were her lover, her slender hands gliding up and down before she skillfully twisted her body and turned upside down on the pole.

That seemed to have impressed the crowd as they threw notes at her before filling their hands with more notes.

"Celine?" I turned quickly when I heard my name being called, and my heart thudded in my chest when I realized who was right behind me.

Chapter 5

I SHOOK MY HEAD AS if to clear it and blinked a few times. "Milano, what are you doing here?" I asked, pleased with the firmness in my voice.

His gaze shifted from my face to my cleavage quickly, and I could feel the small trickles of heat making their way through my body. "I could ask you the same thing."

"Well, Sylvia is my friend. I couldn't miss her first night."

He nodded, a small smile on his face while his dark grey eyes inspected me.

I swallowed. "Did my dad send you to watch me?"

He raised a brow at that. "Does he even know you're here?"

My cheeks blazed. "No."

He chuckled. "I thought so, but to answer your question, no, he didn't, and my next shift is noon tomorrow."

"Ohh," I answered softly.

I looked past Milano's shoulder and saw Jensen and Hector coming up the stairs. My pulse quickened as our gazes met. Their presence commanded the attention of everyone in the room; even couples who were together stopped to unabashedly stare at them.

I pulled in a breath as they approached and mustered my best smile. Hector smiled and moved towards me with a hug that

37

I basked completely in. His musky-citrusy perfume did little to calm me, instead making me more delirious than I already was.

"Hey, Celine," Jensen said as he, too, took his turn to hug me. Heat cascaded through my entire body.

"Hey," I said. "So, all you guys have the night off tonight?" I gawked.

"Yup, unlike your old man who has the huge job of running everything," Hector said.

I smiled. "Well, he wouldn't be here anyway."

Jensen chuckled. "Well, I don't think you'd be either."

"Well, that's true," I agreed.

"So, what do you guys want to drink?" Milano asked while Jensen and Hector plopped down in the red leather sofas behind us.

"Oh, I'll just settle with a club soda for now," I said.

Hector raised his brow. "Well, I'm not drinking heavily either since I have work in the morning." The others nodded in agreement. Milano called over a waitress who wore a skimpy little skirt with a white top she had tucked in. She took our orders, and while she did so, it suddenly dawned on me that I hadn't bothered to greet Skye. Though I had no doubt she was busy, I could have at least let her know I was here. Maybe later, I thought as I positioned myself between the guys. I was right beside Milano, and for a second, I wondered if he'd told the others what had happened. Guys talked to each other, right? Plus, they were friends who worked in the same place. What were the chances?

But Jensen and Hector didn't seem indifferent towards me, so I knew that even if he did, I had nothing to worry about since there was no sign of judgement on their faces.

"Have you ever been to a place like this?" Milano asked me as soon as the drinks came.

There was just something about the looks he gave me now that seemed different than before. Now, each time he looked at me, it felt like I could see the hunger in his gaze and feel the heat of his stare. Whenever our gazes met, my pulse raced, and I knew it was all because of what had happened back at my house.

"No, my first time actually," I said, taking a sip of my soda.

"Mmm, I guess there's a first for everything," he said as he watched me over the rim of his glass. A bolt of heat shot through me at the look in his eyes, and I could tell all this was about what happened in the powder room and the fact he knew I was a virgin.

"Definitely."

"You're still young," Hector added. "You have a lot to experience for the first time."

"You sure do," Jensen said.

I didn't know if it was my mind playing tricks on me, but I just couldn't see this as normal conversation. Maybe my mind had gotten too dirty, and I couldn't differentiate what was actually normal from what wasn't.

"I can't wait," I mumbled.

"What's on your bucket list?" Hector asked.

I rubbed the nape of my neck and pulled in a breath. "I don't think I have one," I lied. But, of course, they didn't know the type of adventure I wanted was nothing like climbing a mountain or jumping out of a plane.

Jensen scoffed. "Everyone has a bucket list."

"What's yours," I pried.

"Well, one is I'd like to travel to every Caribbean country before I turn fifty."

I smiled. "Well, you have almost fifteen years to make that happen. I have a feeling it will."

"You know my age?" Jensen asked.

I laughed. "I've known you guys for almost a year. I know a few things."

"Sounds like you did your research," Hector said, a small smile on his face.

"I kinda did," I admitted.

They chuckled. All eyes were on me, making me feel warm and safe – but most of all, a little aroused.

"Tell us something about you, Celine. Something not many people know," Milano challenged, and I knew what he was getting at. Surely, this wasn't innocent.

I chewed on my bottom lip. "Er... I'm not really... fun. There's nothing interesting about me," I said.

Hector scoffed. "I know for a fact that's not true. A beautiful girl like you has to have her secrets."

My stomach fluttered at the compliment. I was about to open my mouth to talk when a waitress approached with a smile on her face. She went to Milano and whispered something in his ear, and my face flushed from the thought of her flirting with him. Something resembling jealousy surfaced inside me, and I found myself scowling.

Milano raised a brow as he listened, and then he stood. Turning to us, he gestured for us to get up with the flick of his hand.

"What's going on?" Hector asked.

"We're being invited to a private room," he shrugged, glancing at me. "Ladies first."

I swallowed hard and made the first move, slowly moving down the steps with all three men behind me. Something about that made me happy and made me feel more confident than I'd ever been.

The woman led the way through a small passageway and then paused at a door. She glanced at all of us before she shoved it open and stepped to the side. I timidly made my way inside, barely able to see much except for the pole at the front and a king-sized bed with red satin sheets. But the more I observed the space, the more I realized that a few persons were inside seated on couches resembling the one in the VIP section, but with the dim lighting, I couldn't even properly see their faces. That was probably a good thing, I began to realize, as the woman showed us to our seats and then left the room.

"What's going on?" I asked though I had a pretty good idea.

"I think this is mega-VIP," Hector chuckled, and I couldn't help but smile at that.

Soft, sensual music played in the background, filling the entire space. A woman stepped out, completely naked, and my heart skipped a beat. It suddenly occurred to me that this was what Sylvia was talking about.

"Fuck," I muttered under my breath, already feeling the signs of my arousal. My gaze was glued to the woman in front of us. Her skin was pristine and spotless and pale as paper but looked incredibly soft. She was a bit on the chubbier side – a bit thicker than me, but her curves were very shapely. She had wide hips and a flat stomach. Her breasts were full but had a gentle dip before welcoming pink, taut nipples.

Before I was done admiring her, two men stepped forward from each side, both lean, tall, and muscular, with their flaccid cocks dangling in front of them as they walked. I swallowed hard, feeling the heat engulf my body at their appearance. They were similarly built to Jensen, Milano and Hector, but their faces were bare.

"Damn, tonight's definitely gonna be a good night," Hector mumbled in the midst of the silent room. I adjusted myself on the sofa, glanced at the men who were at my side and then at the stage again. One man started to kiss the girl in a deep and passionate kiss while the other, who was behind, massaged her hips and kissed along her neck and shoulders. They were right up on her, and I was sure she could feel their cocks pressing against her. I already wished it was me in that position, and my aching flesh agreed.

They kissed for some time, and the men's cocks twitched to life, hardening in front of her. She reached for one and massaged it in her hands before she broke the kiss and fell to her knees. My heart lurched in my chest again as what was about to happen dawned on me.

Her face was right at his crotch, and she continued to massage his member until it was semi-erect. Still, without being fully hard, he was huge, and as she slipped his length inside her mouth, it filled out the corners of her lips. The guy arched his neck and released a deep moan before he raked his fingers through her hair and urged her on.

I licked my lips, seemingly in a trance, as I looked to the other guy who came closer, handing his cock for her to jack off with her free hand. She captured it skillfully while she sucked on the other one.

I swallowed hard and glanced at Milano, Hector and Jensen, who seemed just as engrossed as I was. Hector even had his back crouched, watching intently.

I knew my panties were soaked, I could feel the dampness between my legs already and knew I'd be drenched by the time this was finished. By the time I glanced back at the stage, the woman was choking on the cock in her mouth while the big, burly man plunged his dick down her throat. Trickles of her saliva began to drain from her lips to the floor, the sloppy sounds echoing in the room. Throughout all this, her pace on the other man had not wavered.

My flesh began to pool with even more juices as I watched, and when I thought she couldn't take a second more or that the guy would come, he pulled her off him and slapped his cock against her face a couple of times until it reddened. She gasped for breath, licking around her lips. The other man took the position of the other, and as she opened her mouth, he slipped his cock inside. He thrusted it to the hilt before he held her at the back of the head with her nose crushed against his pelvis.

After a few seconds, he pulled out, and she gasped for breath – but not for long. His manhood was inside her mouth again in the next second, and he maintained a rhythm of pulling out and then driving back to the hilt. Her drool stretched from her lips to his cock each time he pulled out and went back in each time he filled her mouth.

He groaned animalistically the last time he pulled out and squeezed his cock tight before he lifted her from the floor in one lithe movement. He carried her to the bed as if she weighed nothing and dropped her on it. The girl giggled, spreading her legs to the audience in the process. We were welcomed with the wet, pink view of her cunt.

From the corner of my eye, I saw Hector reach for a glass of water on the table in front of us and take a healthy gulp. I took it a bit further by looking at them more intently and realized, much to my surprise, that they were hard. The bulks in their pants couldn't be mistaken for anything else. I felt my arousal dribbling down my pussy from what I saw, and when Milano looked up at me, I was sure my wetness was soaking my skirt.

A sensuous moan had my gaze back towards the stage, and I realized that one of the men had entered the woman bareback. He was perched above her in a way that allowed us to see her pussy being stuffed from where we were, and I pulled in a breath.

He pumped her slowly at first as if allowing her to get used to the size of his monstrous cock. I wasn't sure how much more I could watch and not get something close to what was happening – if not the exact thing. I glanced around the dimly lit room and saw a couple some yards away kissing each other. The man had his hands up her dress, and she had one leg propped over his while they shared a hungry kiss. Another couple did the same, and I almost felt desperate to copy.

But before I could make a move, Milano placed a hand on my thigh, and I knew then maybe wouldn't be possible for me to get more aroused. His warm hand sent a thousand signals through my body, and I nodded at him, not knowing exactly what I was approving, but it just felt like the right thing to do.

His hand slipped up my bare leg, and I held my breath in anticipation, fearing I'd have a heart attack before anything happened. This wasn't us being alone in a powder room. It was us in public, surrounded by Hector and Jensen – and strangers.

I was burning up and knew I could only be satisfied if I was touched. I parted my legs, willing myself not to look at Hector and Jensen as yet. I didn't want to see their reaction as yet – and somehow, I feared it.

I spread my legs wider, allowing Milano access while I held his gaze. His fingers crept up between my legs, and I felt my pooling arousal continue to spill for him. When his fingers brushed my clothed crotch, I sucked in a breath, and when he slipped my panties to the side, I was sure I was about to come. I mewled softly as he pressed his finger to my crotch. It slipped between my thick folds, and he muttered a curse.

"You're so fucking wet," he muttered under his breath.

I nodded while he used two fingers to caress me, making me more aroused as he swept them over my sensitive clit. I quivered on the sofa and finally managed to tear my gaze away from Milano.

I turned to the other side, where Jensen and Hector were, and realized the shock on their faces.

"Fuck, so this is happening?" Hector asked. My gaze lowered to his bulge, and I nodded, almost salivating about one day seeing the sight of his cock – all three men.

Just then, Milano slipped two fingers inside me, and I gasped, loving the way his fingers smoothly slid inside me. I was so wet it felt like all three cocks would fit inside me all at once, yet the way his fingers filled me, I knew that was impossible.

I leaned into Hector a bit, and he kissed me, capturing my lips almost hungrily. I moaned against him as he took my plump lips and caressed them with his tongue, gently nipping them with his teeth. Milano started to maintain a pace, slipping his fingers as far as my hymen would allow. Hector kissed me, his hands travelling to my chest, where he grabbed one of my breasts and started to caress.

Milano's pace increased, and so did my moans as my body buzzed with pleasure. Jensen, the one left out of the action stood and came in front of me. I shifted a little and Hector and Milano all but stopped what they were doing. Milano pulled out his soaked fingers and Jensen knelt in front of me. My chest started to heave, seeing him in that position while he looked at me with his hungry gaze.

"Do you want this, Celine?" he asked me while his hands traveled up my leg.

I nodded quickly, and he hooked his fingers into my panties and pulled them down my legs. I pulled my skirt a bit further up my waist and spread my thick thighs for them. I could feel Jensen's hot breath against my skin, and just like that, I felt even more of my juices running to soak my pussy.

"God, I love everything about your body," Jensen said, still massaging my thighs with his huge hands. "I've been waiting for a long time to touch you like this..."

I felt breathless. "You have."

"Yes, and to stick my head between these beautiful thighs – taste your sweet pussy." I hadn't expected such words to come from Jensen since I'd never heard him speak so dirty before. But hearing him dirty only spurred my desires even more.

I glanced at Hector. "You guys wanted me?"

"From the very first day we laid eyes on you, Celine, we knew we wanted to touch you – to fucking kiss those sexy, luscious lips of yours. We've long awaited this moment," I confessed.

My voice trembled. "I have, too. I've fantasized about moments like these," I said.

"Tell us more," Jensen insisted before he dipped his head between my thighs and licked from the base of my pussy to the top. My moans robbed me of the words I wanted to say and made my head spin.

"I wanted all three of you to get a share of my virgin pussy," I exclaimed shakily.

Jensen eased up to look at me, his lips wet. "Virgin."

I nodded. "Yeah."

"You've gotta be kidding," Hector said.

I shook my head, and that was all I could do as Jensen licked my pussy again before he latched his mouth to my clit and sucked hard. I moaned hard, my head falling back with my eyes closed. It felt so good to have him down there, his soft lips, his warm tongue, but also his beard that tickled me in the right places and added to the overall appeal.

My eyes fluttered open, and my gaze went to the stage, which I'd forgotten for a moment. The woman was now sandwiched between the two men – one in her pussy and the other in her ass, moving at the same pace while her cries filled the room.

My pussy tingled even more, and with Jensen eating me out like this, I knew it wouldn't be long before I came. Jensen continued to suck and lick me, just before he inserted his two fingers inside me. I reached for Milano's leg and gripped it tight, wanting some sort of support. But he took my hand and placed it on his cock I didn't even realize was out. My gaze went to his manhood, taking note of its bulkiness and the shimmering pink head. I slid my hands over it and massaged him, my small hands almost lost around the girth.

"Lick your palm, baby girl," Milano said. For a second, I didn't know what he meant, but it slowly dawned on me. I licked my palm, making sure it was wet before I started my hand job again.

I looked over to Hector and did the same with my free hand, realizing they were similar in many ways. So far, no one seemed to sport a small cock. I just knew that Jensen's wouldn't be either.

I started to moan as the pace of Jensen's fingers increased. My flesh started to clench around him, and I knew my orgasm wasn't far away. As he continued to suckle on my flesh, the pleasure got more intense, and I knew there was no going back. My flesh convulsed, and with a loud moan, I came quivering – my body seemingly in another dimension as the pleasure crashed into me. I snapped my eyes closed, allowing the sensations to overwhelm me.

Through my haze of pleasure, I felt when Jensen slipped his fingers from me, and my body jolted, still not down from its high. I offered a shaky smile and placed my attention on the stage where the throuple seemed to be finishing off as well. My limbs seemed like putty, and in that moment, I truly didn't know if I had the energy to move.

I looked down at Jensen, Milano and Hector and smiled. They all seemed pleased, too, and I was happy for that.

"How do you feel?" Jensen asked.

"Like this is the best day of my life," I didn't hesitate to say.

They all smiled. "More to come, baby, but maybe next time. It looks like they're over for tonight," Milano said, winking.

As much as my orgasm had been fulfilling, it still felt like there was something else missing, and I knew exactly what it was. There would always be an itch to scratch if I didn't have one of them inside me – their cocks, to be exact. My body still buzzed with anticipation for that to happen, and if I weren't so overwhelmed and exhausted, I would have made a suggestion regarding that.

"Thank you guys so much," I managed as I adjusted my skirt. My cheeks burned bright when I saw Jensen slip my discarded panties into his pockets.

"A little parting gift," he said, and I giggled, nodding.

"Next week, same time?" Hector asked, and I bit my lips, knowing that seemed like eons away, but I also knew they were busy and a moment like this wouldn't present itself again for a long time.

I nodded. They all got up. Milano stretched out a hand, and I placed mine in his as I stood. My knees buckled, and as soon as my thighs touched, I could still feel the juices from my orgasm. Milano led the way back inside the club, and it suddenly felt like a whole new world to me, the noise, the people packed together and the blasting music. I blushed as a few random people glanced at me. I knew they had no idea what had happened, but just the realization of what I'd done made me feel dirty – in the best possible way.

I was surrounded by big, burly men, and that alone made me feel like I was on cloud-nine. What more could I ask for?

Well...

Chapter 6

FOR THE FOLLOWING DAYS, I heard nothing from the guys. They didn't come over, and when I asked Dad how things were going at the hospital, he said everyone was busy with shifts. Although they'd said the weekend, part of me had expected some action in between – kinda like what happened between me and Milano at the house. But I was left to use my imagination and watch porn since I couldn't get the real thing right away.

It felt like my hunger grew more consuming each time I'd gotten a taste of intimacy, and now it felt like I was on the verge of losing my mind. My own fingers couldn't do as great of a job as the others. It was like they'd spend the better part of their lives learning how to touch women in the right places. I didn't doubt that. They were all skilled, but I still burned with an unquenchable thirst that was almost agonizing.

Added to that, Sylvia was gone for the week, and I didn't have anyone to visit and talk to. It was just me all by my lonesome self in the empty house. I could have called Sylvia, but I didn't want to disturb her. I'd thought a week without her wouldn't hurt, but it felt like a pivotal part of my life was missing due to her absence.

The days rolled by quickly, and before I knew it, it was Saturday again. Already, my body was pumping with adrenaline; I couldn't wait for my dreams to finally become reality. That night, I got dressed in a short bodycon dress and headed out. As soon as I got there and secured parking, my cell phone rang, and I realized it was Sylvia. Truth be told, it was always either her or my dad.

"Hey," I said, my gaze focused on the long line outside. This time, though, it was no surprise.

"Hey you, how's everything going? Miss me yet?" she laughed at that.

"Yet? I've missed you ever since you left," I said.

"Aww, I'll be back in a few days, so don't worry, you'll have some company," she said. "Are you at the club yet?"

"Yeah, I actually just got here."

"Great, I have another surprise for you this week," she said, her voice low and soft. Without even seeing her, I knew she was smiling.

"Another surprise?" I questioned with furrowed brows. "What was the first?"

"Last week. I invited the boys," she said.

My eyes widened. "You did?"

She giggled. "I thought you all needed some encouragement."

My cheeks stung. "Wow, you're really out there working behind the scenes," I laughed. "Thank you; last week was amazing."

"I'm glad. This time, if you're up to it, you can lead the show."

"What do you mean?"

"Be the entertainers instead of the spectators."

I gasped. "No way."

"It's up to you, but I'm pretty sure you wished it was you in that position last week, didn't you?"

I bit down on my lips. "Yeah, I did."

"Then you could get up there and be the star of your own show."

"Do you think they'll want to do it?"

"If they sucked your pussy in public, they'll definitely fuck you in public. Plus, the type of people in the room are people I've known for a long time. What happens in there stays there."

I pulled in a breath. "I really wish you were here," I said.

"Would you even be considering this if I was?" she asked.

I snorted. "Probably not."

She chuckled softly. "Just as I thought. But this is your chance, sweetie, make the best of it."

I smiled. "Thank you...for everything."

"Don't mention it. Don't forget to fill me in on all the juicy details tomorrow."

"OMG, goodbye!" I exclaimed.

She laughed loudly. "Have fun, love."

I smiled before I hung up the phone and sighed, pondering over what Sylvia had said. I didn't even know what I expected from tonight. I wanted the thrill, and I wanted the pleasure, but did I ever consider public sex? Tonight? The thought wasn't frightening. In fact, it was exciting to think about, but I didn't know where the others stood. Were they willing to go that far? That was the true puzzle.

I grabbed my purse and went around the back. Sylvia had already told me she'd told security I'd be coming back again, so I didn't have any problems getting in. It felt like deja vu, but this time before I went to the VIP area, I stopped by the bar area to tell Skye hi. She was busy, and it was really hard to mow my way through the thick crowd that surrounded the counter. But she spotted me coming, and a smile graced her face.

"Celine, hey!" she exclaimed above the music.

"Hey. I just stopped to say hi. I'll be up top," I said.

"Oh, nice. Could I get you anything to drink?"

"No, I'm great, but thank you. I'll see you around."

"Definitely," I said before I smiled and made my way back through the sea of people.

I made my way up the small steps, pausing when I saw all three of my father's friends seated in the same chair we'd occupied last week. They were chatting and having drinks, but as if sensing my presence, they looked in my direction and saw me standing there. Milano eased back in his chair, his gaze blatantly trailing along every inch of me with a look in his eyes that was no short of desirous.

I smiled as I took a step forward. "I didn't know you guys were already here," I said.

"We didn't want to keep the lady waiting," Jensen said, standing to greet me. He took a step forward and kissed me on the lips – much to my surprise. It reminded me of where his lips had been a week ago, and desire shot through me instantly.

I kissed him back gently, and just as I felt like I needed more, he broke the kiss. Milano stood and stepped towards me, and my heart raced when he dipped his head to do the same. Then it was Hector who kissed me more gruffly. Once we broke apart, I realized some people were watching us, but I didn't feel any kind of embarrassment; I felt proud. Proud to be in the presence of such hot men who wanted me as much as I wanted them.

I could see the envy and shock in some of the women's faces and couldn't help my smile.

Just as I was about to take a seat, the waitress from the week before ushered us to follow her. Milano led the way this time, and I followed behind him, staring at his broad back while my body continued to flood with heat. She guided us to the room, which had fewer people than the night before. A naked woman was dancing on the pole that was there, but the bed beside it was untouched. I swallowed hard as I took a seat, thinking back to what Sylvia had said.

"Are you okay?" Milano asked.

I quickly nodded. "Yeah, I'm great."

"If you're not comfortable with something, all you have to do is say it, baby. It's your world," he winked.

I blushed. "Thank you."

"You look amazing, by the way, Celine," Hector dropped in.

"Definitely. Those curves and juicy, plump lips... I can't wait to have it wrapped around my cock," Jensen said. His voice was low and husky.

My core pooled with heat at his words. "I've never done that before," I confessed.

"Hmm, a virgin pussy and a virgin mouth?" he said.

"Is that ass of yours just as untouched?" Hector asked, and I almost gasped.

"You don't mind having all holes filled, do you?"

I shook my head. "I want you guys all over me?"

Milano smiled. "And do you think you can handle that, baby? Three hefty men like us fucking all your tight little holes?"

I swallowed. "I can." I hoped that was true.

He smiled. "We love a confident little minx."

Just then, my gaze shifted to the woman on the stage – she was a slender one. As she slid down the pole, she smiled at the crowd before her gaze flashed to me. My heart lurched in my chest when she called me up with the flicker of her finger.

"What?" I said, knowing there was no way she would hear what I said. I glanced at Milano and the others, and all they did was smile.

The girl waved me up again, and I froze, not knowing what to do. Somehow, I'd expected something like this, but now that it was actually happening, it still left me shocked.

Milano leaned into me, his lips almost brushing my ear. "Do you wanna go up there? Spread your thick thighs and allow us to fuck you the way you want – all these people watching?"

I shivered. "I do."

"Then let's go," he said.

I swallowed as I looked at them. "And this is something you all want to do?" I asked.

"There's nothing more we'd love, Celine," Jensen said.

I smiled. My heart swelled with happiness, knowing that they wanted me – wanted me in every which way possible.

I got up and pulled at the hem of my dress, though I knew that in a short while it would be gone from my body. The walk to the front seemed endless. I blinked a few times when I stepped into the light and gazed at the few people in the room. Luckily there wasn't anyone I recognized, but Sylvia had already told me that no one here would talk, and I believed her. I trusted her.

The naked woman left through the back, and it dawned on me that this was it. I was left to entertain the crowd just as the woman the previous week had done. I was a virgin and didn't have any experience up my sleeve, but I trusted that the guys would make me feel great, and I would make them feel great – and that was all that mattered.

Chapter 7

MILANO STEPPED TOWARDS me and broke the tension by kissing me. I kissed him back with as much need, pulling against his tongue. He wrapped his arms around me and pulled me closer to him. While we kissed, I could feel the heat that radiated from him onto me and his musky perfume, which all added to the overall appeal that made my brain putty.

I kissed him back, and just like that, the world faded around us. All I could concentrate on was this fantasy I'd wanted for so long, and I was finally living it. I could already feel the juices flowing from my pussy and into my panties. With just one kiss, I was soaked, and as they passed me around to kiss the others, I knew my essence would be trailing to my legs in a matter of seconds.

As I kissed Jensen, Hector stood behind me. I almost shivered when his fingers touched my naked skin. He pulled my zipper down, and then he pulled the dress over my shoulders. I broke free from Jensen when it fell to the floor, leaving me in just my panties and my bra. They all stood there watching, and my heart swelled with emotions.

"Take it all off," Hector instructed as he undid the buttons to his shirt, eyes still focused on me regardless.

I stood before the crowd, and for the first time in a long time, I was self-conscious of my curves. I'd never been naked in front of anyone before. But I wanted this, so I reached for the clipper at the front of my bra and unhooked it. The weight of my heavy breasts dipped in my chest, and I sucked in a breath when they all cursed in unison.

That gave me a boost in confidence, and I continued to strip myself, slowly pulling my black, lace panties down my legs. I stepped out of them and stood there, as naked as the day I was born, with my hair flowing down my back.

"You're perfect, Celine," Hector said. "Chef's kiss."

I glanced at their reaction and saw the way they hastened to strip themselves. Soon after, they were all naked alongside me, all having toned, bulky muscles and hung cocks that were already hard. Milano had a tattoo of a dragon on his right pecs, but the others were spotless. Hector was hairy around the crotch area, while the others were shaved.

"They're so big; damn," I heard one woman from the crowd exclaim. My gaze shifted to find her with her hands against her chest, squeezing her large breasts under her clothes.

I licked my lips and swallowed as wetness pooled in my mouth. They looked good enough to eat. Hector approached the bed and called me over. I realized for the first time there were a few things on it – a bottle of lube and a butt plug.

"Lay across my lap, Sweets," Hector said, his throbbing cock long and thick between his legs. I did as asked, feeling the bulge in my stomach. Jensen came up towards me, wagging his length in his hand and towards my face. I licked my lips as I peered at the gleaming head.

"All yours," he said, directing it towards my lips. I reached for it, held it and licked across the tip. The saltiness took me by surprise, but I could also taste the tinge of soap he'd used.

Curious to know about the full experience, I licked from the base of his cock all the way to the tip – going off what I'd seen in porn. The more I did it, the more I enjoyed it, and before long, I inserted the tip in my mouth and sucked on it, gaining a moan from Jensen.

"Just like that, sweetheart. Use those lips to pleasure my cock," he said, raking his hands through my hair. I took him in deeper, taking in a few more inches and enjoying the feel of my lips gliding along his veiny cock.

Meanwhile, Hector spread my ass cheeks and squeezed them into his hands. As he massaged them, my juices overflowed from my pussy. As I tried my best to get more of Jensen's cock into my mouth, Hector ran his hand over the expanse of my ass. He caressed my inner thighs, his finger brushing against my quim, and I moaned. The graze of my flesh must have set him off because his hands paused before he parted my flesh further and stared at me. After a series of profanities, he dragged his fingers along my lips and smeared my juices all over my second-hole. I mewled with pleasure as his fingers fondled with my rosebud.

"I thought I'd need the lube, but you're as wet as a river." He continued to spread the juices from my pussy all over my second hole, and I moaned, while Jensen's cock slipped deeper down my throat. I was a slobbering mess, but his moans told me he liked it, and so I continued despite myself.

Hector continued to rub his thumb against my bud. He pressed the tip against my second hole, and I paused, feeling a slight bit of pressure as he pressed gently. His thumb slid inside, and I moaned as my snug asshole clenched around his intruding finger. There wasn't any word I could use to describe how this felt, but it was amazing. Hector pressed his finger deeper, and I squealed as I felt the pressure heighten.

A spurt of cold liquid hit my ass, and it didn't take me long to realize it was the lube. As it slid down between my cheeks, Hector pulled out his finger and spread it all over before he popped his thumb back in again.

Jensen's cock slid deeper down my throat, and my eyes watered, the urge to cough taking control of me. He began to thrust in and out of my slobbering mouth while Hector twisted his finger around in my ass.

"God, that feels good," Jensen said, gripping my head even tighter and started to lunge his cock further in it. He pulled out for me to catch my breath, and I coughed and swallowed. Not giving me a second more, his slipped his manhood past my lips again and sighed heavily as he fucked my throat.

Hector's finger popped out again, this time longer than the last time. I felt something against my ass again and knew it wasn't his finger. It felt harder and colder, and my heart raced. He pressed it against my opening, and I moaned since words failed me.

"Relax, sweetie," Hector said as he pressed harder. I listened to what he had to say, and a second later, the toy slipped past my flesh and settled inside me. The feeling was new, my ass felt full, and my pussy just couldn't stop flowing. As if reading my thoughts, Hector slipped his fingers inside and tipped me closer towards the edge.

My wetness was loud as Hector moved his fingers back and forth, and my cheeks burned while being stuffed with Jensen's cock. His pace hadn't slowed, and my throat burned with the consistent pounding. I didn't want to disappoint, though, and

I loved the feel of having him inside my mouth – pleasuring himself to the feel of my lips.

"Where do you want my cum?" he asked, still bucking back and forth and sounding breathless. "Your face?" he asked. "Mouth?" I nodded at that since I couldn't say anything, and he sucked in a breath.

With one final thrust of his hips, he grunted, and I felt the hot blast of cum spurt to the back of my throat. It triggered a cough, and luckily, Jensen was just in time to remove his length from my mouth. With my mouth full, I coughed but tried to swallow some. Being no pro, most of it sputtered from my lips and down my chin, filling me with a bit of embarrassment.

I glanced at the crowd who had their eyes peered on what was going on, some of them making out – while some were blatantly fucking, and I knew I had to be doing a good job.

"You took that cock like a champ, Cel," Jensen said as he squeezed the remainder of his cum from his cock. The reassurance made me smile and lick my lips, teasing Jensen a little.

I was pulled from the bed after that and with my mind reeling, I later realized it was Milano who had me in his arms. I clung to him, seeing his darkened green eyes that were filled with lust.

He placed me on my back, and I parted my legs for him, the butt plug still lodged in my ass.

Chapter 8

"ARE YOU READY TO WORK this pretty little pussy?" Milano asked, rubbing his monstrous cock in his hand.

"I'm ready," I said breathlessly, knowing there still had to be some of Jensen's cum still left on my mouth, but I didn't mind, and Milano didn't seem to mind either.

"No way that'll fit," one man said from the crowd, a short chuckle following his words. My cheeks stung at his statement, but rather than feeling discouraged and shy, I was eager to prove him wrong.

I turned my head to the side to see who had said it and saw a man of bulk, but certainly not as tall as the guys. He met my gaze, and a smirk curled his lips, but throughout all of this, he still had his long, slender cock in his hand, jerking off at the sight of us.

I smiled and pulled my breasts into my hands, crushing them together before I pulled at my nipples. I writhed on the bed while my ass clenched the butt plug tighter.

"You can't wait, can you? You're so eager to be fucked – to have more cocks inside of you."

"Gosh, I'm so wet for it. My pussy is ready," I heard myself saying, emboldened by my arousal.

He crawled between my legs and dipped his mouth to my breasts. He sucked on my nipples, grazing his teeth over them and causing me to gasp. He crawled further up, straddling me with his cock resting between my breasts. Our gazes met, and I watched with bated breath as he opened his mouth and caused his saliva to drop to his cock.

"Hold your breasts together like you did before," he instructed, and I did as asked, smashing his phallus between my mounds. He began to thrust his hips, and I moaned endlessly as his hardened manhood slipped back and forth between my breasts. Milano bared his teeth and continued to thrust until I thought he'd come.

Suddenly, he pulled out, and I gasped as he went to position himself between my legs again. He looked up at me, and our gazes met.

"Don't worry, baby, I'll make you feel the best you've ever felt," he said. He pried my legs further apart and gripped my thighs firmly. I held my breath when he pressed his tip against my entrance, parting my lips.

Through the corner of my eye, I saw a man approach the stage. He already had his cock in hand, pulling it to life with his face flustered and the buttons of his shirt loose. His eyes were peered where Milano's cock was – right at my pussy. He swallowed and then looked to Milano and me – the look in his eyes like a plea.

I sucked in a breath seeing how people were behaving over us. Milano inched a bit closer, stretching my pussy with his bulky cock. He paused just before he reached the barrier, and I bit my lips, nodding as I gave him the go-ahead. Holding my legs apart, Milano thrust himself inside of me, and a cry ripped from my mouth as he broke the layer of my virginity and drove all the way home. My burning pussy clenched him hard, and more pain riddled my body as my tender flesh clung to his hardness. He paused and rubbed my inner thighs, trying to give me some amount of comfort while allowing my center to get used to his size.

"Fuck, that's hot," the stranger from the crowd announced, his voice ragged as he worked his cock faster in his hand.

When the feeling of discomfort slowly dissipated, I nodded, blinking away the stinging in my eyes.

"Are you good?" Milano asked.

I whimpered. "You promised?"

"Yes," he reassured. "This is only for a minute, but I promise you, at the end of this, you'll always be begging for more of this cock."

I nodded, and just like that, he went deeper, moving slower. With the plug still in my ass, it felt like I was cut open and stuffed with the largest filling. I was still amazed at how Milano fit; he was still so big, and I was so small – virgin small. But here he was, with his cock slipping back and forth in my tender pussy, which quickly started to ignore the aches and focus on the pleasure.

Hector, done being a spectator to me losing my innocence, climbed onto the bed and came towards me. He lowered his lips to mine, and I kissed him eagerly, wanting more comfort than I currently had. He kissed me back with just as much fervor while his hand slid down my heaving stomach. He caressed my flesh as he kissed me, moving from my tender breasts to my belly button and vice-versa.

The pleasure started to build, and the stinging faded, now overcome by the new feeling of arousal that washed over me. As Hector's hand trailed over my stomach, I quivered, and on impulse, my walls clenched tightly onto Milano's cock, shooting a new burst of pleasure inside me. I moaned, and just then, Hector's fingers found my clit. As Milano continued to thrust back and forth inside me, he flicked my swollen clit, making the pleasure ten times more profound.

"Yes," I said, tearing my lips away from Hector's and directing my gaze to Milano, who had his eyes fixated on where and how our bodies joined.

"A bit faster, please," I requested almost breathlessly.

Without an ounce of hesitation, Milano increased his pace, piercing me deeper and harder. At one point, it felt like his cock rubbed against the vibrator in my ass, and I squealed. I knew only a thin layer separated the two, which made this so intense and intimate.

"You should see my cock between these juicy thighs," Milano said, glancing at me. "I know this picture will stay with me forever," he continued. "My huge cock filling this small pussy, your lost virginity, how fucking wet you get for me. I swear I'm the luckiest man alive, baby girl."

I clenched around him, and only then did I realize I liked the dirty talk. I liked knowing what they thought as they pleasured me – and as I pleasured them.

"Yes," I said.

"You like being fucked like this, Celine? A room full of people watching your pussy being stretched by my long, thick cock."

I nodded. "Yes, please. Fuck me even harder."

"Fuck her harder!" someone from the crowd agreed.

He slammed into me, and I cried out loudly, throwing my head back as pleasure and a bit of pain crashed into me. Milano pulled back, dragging his long cock almost all the way out before he pounded into me again. And that was the order of the day as he fucked me, making me scream with each thrust.

"Fuck, you're tight," he muttered between clenched teeth, his grip tightening on my legs.

Moans filled the room – not only mine but a chorus of uneven cries from people who watched me. As my body jerked on the bed, my eyes went to the crowd and what they were doing. The man was still right at the bed with his cock in his hand, his gaze focused on the sight of Milano plowing my pussy. His teeth were bared as he worked his cock, a single vein protruding in his forehead that told me he wouldn't last long.

Another man had his woman over a chair, pounding her from behind, while her large breasts dangled with every thrust, the slapping sounds of their skin echoing in the room.

Hector reached for my pussy again and started to thrash my clit while Milano went to town inside me. I thrashed my head from side to side and writhed on the bed, my flesh gripping Milano tightly as he continued to ram into me. The sensations were too much – too good, and I screamed, my pussy gripping him even tighter.

My words were broken and indecipherable as he bucked into me, and a rush of pure bliss cascaded over my entire body. With my mouth hung open, my body rose to a high that was almost blinding. I came hard, my body quivering. A warm rushing sensation flowed from my center and spilled onto my legs, soaking the bed. I blinked a few times and realized I'd squirted. My body continued to tremble, and my inner walls clenched on nothing when Milano pulled out. My chest heaved as I watched Milano, still between my legs. He jerked his cock several times before the thick burst of his cum spilled above my pussy. I moaned hard as it sluiced down my slit and into my open pussy.

"Fuckkk," Milano exclaimed throatily, still holding his cock. With shaking hands, he inserted himself inside me again and sighed heavily as his cock slipped past my walls. I cried out again, my over-stimulated core still not over my orgasm.

Milano thrust in me a few times, baring his teeth, his body bucking impulsively. I lay there spent, as I felt his cock hardening to life inside me again.

Another grunt filled the room as well as a disjointed cry. Through the haze which surrounded me, I realized the man from the audience came as well, his face contorting in a million different emotions as his cum spurted from his cock. I flinched, thinking it was going to touch me, but instead, it landed on the bed, just inches away from my skin.

Shivering, he pulled himself up from his stupor and slowly walked back to his seat.

MILANO PEELED ME OFF the bed several minutes later. Though my limbs still felt like jello, the mental note I'd made that more was to come filled me with a surge of energy. He laid on his back this time with his length held upright. I climbed on top of him and pierced my used core with it. A gush of his cum oozed from my pussy as he raised his hip to get deeper inside me. I sighed, closing my eyes as the familiar feeling of his swollen cock invaded my senses yet again.

He moved inside me until Hector came behind me. Milano paused as Hector got himself situated. I tried my best to relax when he polished more lube over my ass and then pressed the tip of his dick to my entrance. The pressure felt even more intense and was much greater than the plug. My ass stung as Hector shoved his length in my ass. The rim of my hole burned from the penetration, but Hector added more lube as he steadily settled himself.

"Ahh, that's it. Beautiful," he said as he shoved himself in an inch deeper. I was crying out, but Milano kissed along my mouth and my cheeks, trying to comfort me as Hector had done just minutes ago. I kissed him to distract myself from the pain – trying my best to concentrate on the pleasure I received from his lips and his cock.

Hector began to move gently; there wasn't much Milano could do in this case. He'd have his moment, but yet his cock still felt so incredibly good inside my drenched pussy. I couldn't believe I was this stuffed. When Jensen came over, I knew there was still room for more. I perched up a little and reached for his cock, pulling it into my hands, stroking him before I took him into my mouth.

They all moved at different paces, which was maddening as much as satisfying. I felt like I was about to lose my mind at the immense pleasure zinging through my body. I moaned, feeling like a used little slut that they made me.

"You like that, huh – you like being stuffed with all three cocks," Milano whispered, and I moaned in response.

People from the crowd came closer, realizing there was nothing wrong in doing so. We were surrounded by both men and women – mostly men – who looked at me as if I were a prize. Men who looked at me as if they wanted to take the guys' spot and have their way with me. Those who didn't have their women to fuck watched with focus as they pulled their cocks into their hands and groaned deeply as Milano, Hector and Jenson had their way with my holes.

The feeling was overwhelming; every sensory organ was on overdrive. My body buzzed with a new type of feeling I'd never experienced before. I was high on pleasure, and as the dam broke within me, I came for the second time, squirting my juices all over their cocks while I screamed Milano's name. As I lay on top of him, exhausted, I felt the warm sprays of cum all over me and smiled as I basked in the feeling, knowing it wasn't only from those who fucked me but those who watched as well.

I gasped as Milano's flaccid cock slipped from inside me, followed by a dollop of his thick, creamy cum. He kissed my cheeks, still moaning against my ear while his hands trailed down my sides, spreading cum like lotion all over my skin.

I smiled; there was simply nothing better than this. Finally, my fantasies were now reality.

Epilogue

9 months later

"ARE YOU SURE YOU DON'T want me to take you?" my dad asked as I pulled my suitcase from the living room.

I sighed. "Dad, I'm positive. I know you're busy, and I understand that. Trust me, I'm not upset about it."

He sighed as well and scratched his head. "Okay, fine, but call me as soon as you arrive at the airport and right after you land."

"Of course, I will. That goes without saying," I said, smiling.

He smiled back and moved towards me. "I love you."

"And I love you. Now go save some lives; I'll be fine."

He chuckled. "I can't believe Milano left, and now you're going too. Who's next?' he said, throwing up his hands in frustration.

I tried my best not to blush at the mention of Milano's name. "Well, maybe we'll bump into each other in L.A.," I smiled.

"I hope so. At least I'll be assured there's someone there to keep an eye out."

I cleared my throat. "I'll be just fine, Dad."

He hugged me. "You've been such an amazing person and daughter all your life ... I'm so proud of you. I have no doubt that this new journey will be great for you, and you're gonna do great."

I smiled as I hugged him tighter. "I will, Dad and thank you for being an amazing Dad."

He chuckled. 'Thanks Sweetie."

A car honked outside, and I glanced towards the window. "That must be Sylvia," I said, pulling in a breath. "I'd better get going."

He reached for my suitcases and helped me to get them outside. He greeted Sylvia who waved and loaded my things into the back of her jeep. I hugged my dad one last time before I hopped in beside Sylvia in the front seat and waved at him.

"I'll call you."

"Please do," he said.

Sylvia honked and then drove off. I watched him in the rearview until his image disappeared, and then I sighed, already feeling a tad bit sad.

"I'm going to miss him so much," I muttered.

"Yeah, you will, but you'll also have an amazing time in college," she said.

"You think so?"

"Of course. College is fun; it's where you have the most sex and have the most fun," she laughed.

I scoffed. "I'm not too sure about the sex part."

She laughed. "Oh, I forgot, you're locked in."

I rolled my eyes but couldn't help my blush. "Please..."

"I'm happy for you, though. You're one of the lucky ones."

I grinned. "I suppose you're right."

"You know I am."

I sighed. "Do you think it'll work though? What if he gets tired of me or no longer finds me attractive. There's tons of supermodels in LA – some that he could easily get..."

"None of them is you. You're the full package, love, and I don't know what it'll take for you to realize that."

I smiled. "I don't know what my life would be like without you," I said.

She smiled. "I think about the same thing sometimes."

I burst out laughing, swatting her on the leg. "That's where you were supposed to say 'I don't know what my life would be like without you too,'" I jabbed at her.

Sylvia grinned. "You already know."

"I'll miss you, though, but you said you'd visit, right?"

"Of course. At least as much as I can. And who knows, maybe one day I'll open up a club there, too."

"Now that's a great idea," I said.

The ride to the airport seemed short for the very first time since traveling. I said my goodbyes to Sylvia, feeling the weight of our goodbyes against my chest. My lips quivered, and tears threatened to spill, but I quickly waved and turned my head away from Sylvia as I boarded the flight. I couldn't believe I was leaving two of my favorite people behind, but I also looked towards what I would be met with moving forward. I was torn between feeling excited and sad – none outweighed the other. I wished I was fortunate to have it all, But UCLA had been my dream college ever since I was a kid. Plus, it wouldn't be forever – just a time.

I used the plane ride to reflect on all I had and all I was fortunate to gain over these past months. I was optimistic about the future and proud of myself for all that I achieved. It was really just onward from here.

When the plane landed, and I got my suitcases, I looked around the crowded area, waiting to see a familiar face.

Milano stood above the crowd with his domineering presence and a smile splitting his face as soon as he saw me. My heart pranced with joy, and I giggled as I let go of my suitcases and ran to him. His chuckle almost echoed in the air, and I squealed softly as I crashed into his arms and took a hearty whiff of his familiar perfume. It had only been a week since I'd last seen him, but it truly felt like forever.

"Hey you," he said as he lowered his head and kissed me softly on the lips. I melted into him and kissed him back with as much hunger and lust that I felt.

He chuckled. "Well damn, I missed you, too."

I blushed hard when he lowered his head to my ear and whispered, "And I miss that tight pussy of yours, too. I can't wait to give it its welcome-home gift."

I grinned. "I hope it's ready..."

"For you... always."

I smiled as I tipped to kiss him again. He moved past me and collected my luggage, and we walked to his car.

"How was your flight?"

"It was good – I couldn't wait to see you."

"I'm glad to hear it; happy you didn't get cold feet," he teased.

"Never," I was quick to say.

"Do you want to head to your dorm first or my apartment?"

"Which one will have me on your dick faster?" I asked.

Milano raised a brow, and his eyes darkened. "My apartment – definitely."

I grinned, and he laughed. I wished I'd get to live with him, but we'd later decided that having two separate places would be the best thing. After all, he and my dad were still friends, and if he visited, me being there would bring up questions considering he knew nothing of our relationship.

Maybe one day when the relationship was a bit older, I'd tell him, but I couldn't risk it now. It would pose too many questions, and I didn't want to explain to him how I fell for his friend in a matter of days.

Some things would just have to remain a secret until it wasn't.

I looked across at Milano in the driver's side and smiled. "I love you."

He reached for my hand and returned the smile. "I love you more."

LIKE SHORT, RED-HOT BDSM AND MENAGE STORIES?
CHECK OUT OUR MEGA BUNDLE DEAL?

Over 500 pages *for Only $2.99 or Free for KU & Prime Members.*
Each book is sold for $2.99 or $0.99 individually. A no-brainer deal. Grab yours.
EROTIC DADDY BUNDLE[1]

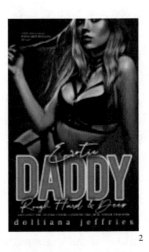

2

CLICK HERE TO DOWNLOAD[3]

Over *500 pages* of Scorching Erotic Stories.
Themes in these stories include: ***BDSM, Menages, Forbidden, Rough Older Men, First Time Brats, Multiple Entries and more.***
Don't miss out on this sizzling collection, download your copy and enjoy some hot, naughty fun tonight. **Get your copy HERE[4]**

LIKE EROTIC ROMANCE NOVELLAS? THEN CHECK OUT IZZIE'S[5] 10 BOOKS for 1 MEGA DEAL?

Only $2.99 or Free for KU & Prime Members for our 10 Novellas Collection
Each book is sold for $2.99 or $0.99 individually. A no-brainer deal. Grab yours.

---

2. https://www.amazon.com/dp/B0C4X5X1ZJ

3. https://www.amazon.com/dp/B0C4X5X1ZJ

4. https://www.amazon.com/dp/B0C4X5X1ZJ

5. https://www.amazon.com/s?k=izzie+vee

10 NOVELLAS COLLECTION[6]

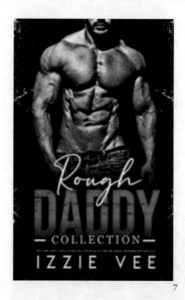

[CLICK HERE TO DOWNLOAD](#)[8]

AN EXTRA STEAMY 10 BOOKS BOX SET

Get the first 10 stories in this series in one quick download.
These stories are insta-love, fast paced standalones that can be read in any order. All are extremely steamy and have a HEA ending.
Some of the themes are age-gap/older man younger woman romance, enemies to lovers, bully romance, grumpy boss, huge mountain man and more ...

List of stories inside:

1. Daddy's Taboo Family-Friend.
2. Possessive Alpha-Daddy
3. Daddy's Bully-Heir
4. Off-Limits Coach Daddy
5. Daddy's Little Birthday Girl

---

6. https://www.amazon.com/dp/B0BVC73GP3

7. https://www.amazon.com/dp/B0BVC73GP3

8. https://www.amazon.com/dp/B0BVC73GP3

6. My Roommate's Sexy Daddy

7. Huge Mountain Daddy

8. Grumpy Christmas Mountain Man

9. MC Daddy Possessive Biker

10. Big Brother's Quarterback Friend.?

<u>Get your copy HERE</u>[9]

LIKE REVERSE HAREM ROMANCE? THEN CHECK OUT THIS HOT REVERSE HAREM BOX SET MEGA DEAL?

Only $2.99 or Free for KU & Prime Members. Over 1,000 pages!

<u>REVERSE HAREM BOX SET</u>[10]

11

<u>CLICK HERE TO DOWNLOAD</u>[12]

9. https://www.amazon.com/dp/B0BVC73GP3

10. https://www.amazon.com/dp/B0CHK5JZF4

11. https://www.amazon.com/dp/B0CHK5JZF4

MORE THAN ONE PLEASE! WHY CHOOSE?

Get ready to devour these three yummy full-length novels about triple alphas sharing, all in one scorching box set! ❤

These alpha men are dominant and outnumber their women always.

And each innocent woman melts into a dripping puddle by these harem of sexy alpha men.

One-click now to steam up your Kindle all night long!

<u>Get your copy HERE</u>[13]

Let's connect.

Get this book for **FREE**[14] when you sign up for our newsletter.

DARK & FILTHY!

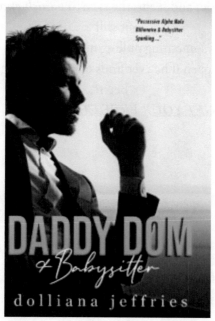

15

<u>CLICK HERE TO GET FOR FREE</u>[16]

WHEN BREAKING RULES LEADS TO BE BROKEN IN.

Older, filthy rich with a ***dark mystery*** to him.

No wonder he had rules. Well, just one rule.

Only one simple rule while working at his mansion.

The perks for working with him are wonderful, plus the pay is great.

A much-needed perk for a ***young college*** student like me.

Then why am I so drawn to break my boss's only rule?

He's stern, strict and seems the type to ***punish and discipline***, but still ...

There's something pulling me. To break his rule.

What will happen if he ever finds out what a naughty girl I've been?

GET YOUR FREE COPY HERE[17]

---

15. https://www.subscribepage.com/b5r0y8

16. https://www.subscribepage.com/b5r0y8

17. *https://www.subscribepage.com/b5r0y8*

Made in the USA
Thornton, CO
05/31/24 10:57:23